Dedicated to my mother, Georgina, without whom
this book wouldn't exist. Also to my father, Stephen, my sister,
Louisa, and my husband, Tom, for their endless support.

BIG PICTURE PRESS

First published in the UK in 2020 by Big Picture Press,
an imprint of Bonnier Books UK,
The Plaza, 535 King's Road, London, SW10 0SZ
www.templarco.co.uk/big-picture-press
www.bonnierbooks.co.uk

1 3 5 7 9 10 8 6 4 2

ISBN 978-1-78741-384-9

This book was typeset in Cabrito Didone
The illustrations were created with watercolour
and ink and finished digitally

Edited by Carly Blake
Designed by Olivia Cook & Marty Cleary
Production by Neil Randles

Printed in China

Sarah Maycock

Sometimes
I feel ...

BPP

Sometimes

I feel as

BIG

as a

Bear.

But there will always
be someone bigger
than me and sometimes
I will feel small.

Sometimes
I feel as
HAPPY
as a
Lark.

But not all days can be filled with song . . .

. . . and sometimes I will need time
before I can join in with the chorus.

Sometimes
I feel as
STRONG
as an
Ox.

But the days that leave me
worn out and weary
will make me stronger tomorrow.

Sometimes
I feel as

BUSY

as a

Bee.

But slowing down to see the beauty all around me is time just as well spent.

Sometimes

I feel as

BRAVE

as a

Lion.

But when the roar of the storm
seems frightening . . .

. . . I know it will pass
and so will my fear.

Sometimes
I feel as

CUNNING

as a

Fox.

But when I'm too clever
for my own good,
I get caught out.

Sometimes I feel as **HUNGRY** as a **Horse.**

But stopping when
I've had enough . . .

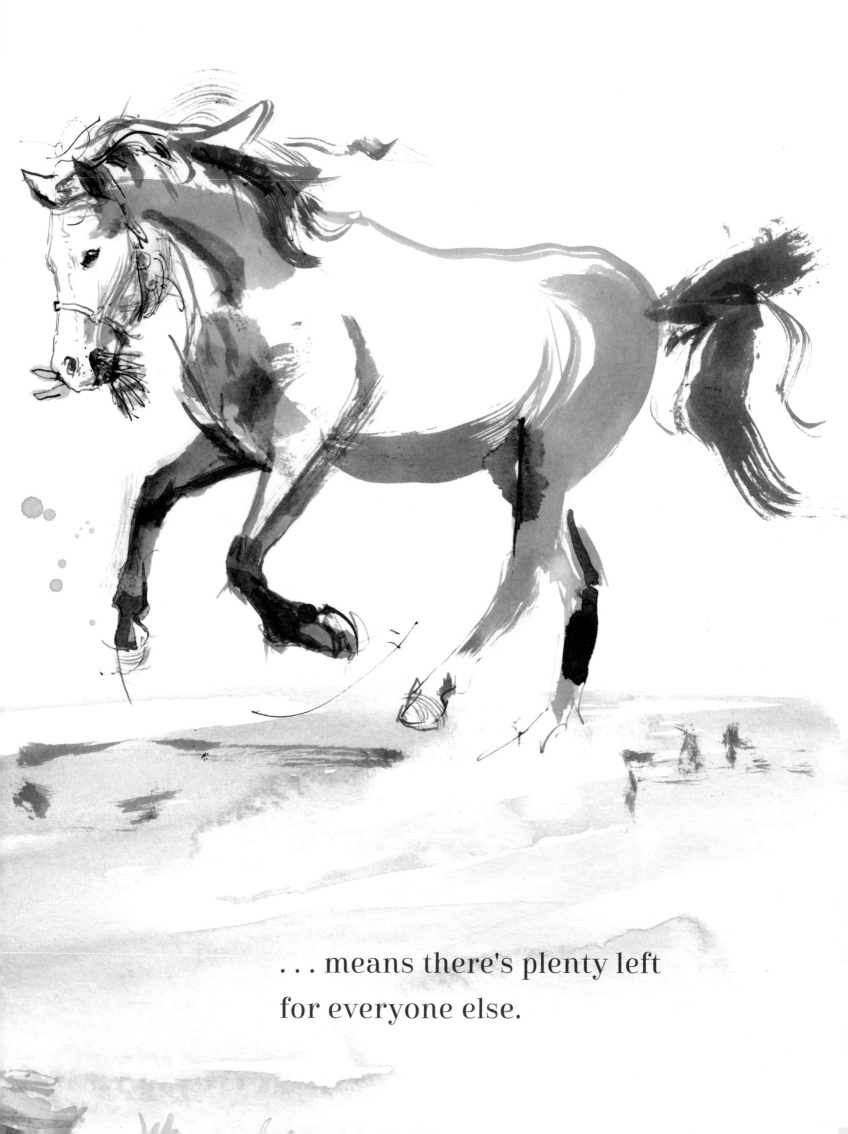

. . . means there's plenty left
for everyone else.

Sometimes
I feel as

CuRiOuS

as a
Cat.

But it's impossible to know
the answers to everything . . .

. . . and sometimes I have
to give my mind a rest.

Sometimes
I feel as

BLIND

as a

Bat.

But when the way
ahead is unclear . . .

. . . following my
instincts will help me
choose the right path.

Sometimes
I feel as
TIMID
as a
Mouse.

But if I stand tall, I can
find my inner courage . . .

. . . and come
to feel . . .

. . . as
BIG
as a
Bear.

A note from the artist

This book began its life in 2011 as my final year project at Kingston University. I wanted to explore the universal nature of animals and how we can relate them to our own experiences and characteristics. In each animal I painted, I saw a feeling that at face value seemed simple, but was there was another side? In looking closer, there is empathy, and in relating, there is self-awareness.

Animals provide an endless way to explore my favourite media, ink and watercolour. I spent time drawing at London Zoo and working from nature documentaries to really see how they move and love thinking about how swooping brush marks could capture a living form. I will never tire of drawing animals.

Sarah Maycock